THERE'S A LITTLE BIT OF ME IN JAMEY

Diana M. Amadeo

pictures by Judith Friedman

Albert Whitman & Company Niles, Illinois

For Len, Angie, Tony, and our 1989 addition. D.M.A.

For Mark Johnson, with many thanks. J.F.

Library of Congress Cataloging-in-Publication Data

Amadeo, Diana.
  There's a little bit of me in Jamey / Diana Amadeo;
illustrated by Judith Friedman.
       p. cm.

  Summary: Brian, whose younger brother Jamey has
leukemia, feels frightened, confused, and neglected by his
parents; but he finds some comfort when he donates bone
marrow to his brother.
  ISBN 0-8075-7854-1 (lib. bdg.)
  [1. Leukemia—Fiction. 2. Transplantation of organs,
tissues, etc.—Fiction. 3. Brothers—Fiction.] I. Friedman,
Judith, 1945-   ill. II. Title.
PZ7.A4915Th 1989   88-20544
[E]—dc19   CIP
                                                            AC

Text © 1989 by Diana M. Amadeo
Illustrations © 1989 by Judith Friedman
Published in 1989 by Albert Whitman & Company,
5747 W. Howard Street, Niles, Illinois 60648
Published simultaneously in Canada by
General Publishing, Limited, Toronto

A Note from the Author

According to the American Cancer Society, each year over six thousand children in the United States under the age of fourteen are diagnosed as having cancer. These malignancies account for the greatest number of deaths by disease of children between the ages of three and fourteen.

There are eight main types of childhood cancers, all with one common denominator—the uncontrolled growth of abnormal body cells. Improvements in therapy have increased children's survival rates significantly. Twenty-five years ago, most children with cancer died. Now, thanks to radiation, chemotherapy, and bone-marrow replacement, many more live.

There's a Little Bit of Me in Jamey was inspired by my experiences as a registered nurse working with sick children. Young cancer patients as well as their siblings, parents, and friends need to be reassured that feelings of fear, confusion, and anger are normal reactions to the disease. While the character of Brian is fictional, he is based on the many brave boys and girls who step forward to donate a little bit of themselves in hopes of saving a brother's or sister's life.

Diana M. Amadeo, R.N.

When I woke up, the house was quiet. Jamey, my little brother, wasn't in the bed beside mine.

"Jamey!" I called. "Mom, Dad!"

No one answered.

Jamey's baseball cards were scattered all over the floor. Usually he keeps them safely tucked under his pillow. It looked as if Jamey had gone somewhere in a hurry.

I ran downstairs to the kitchen. Grandma was there, stirring oatmeal. She gave me an extra-strong hug.

"Where is everybody?" I asked.

Grandma frowned. "Jamey got sick again during the night. Your mom and dad took him to the hospital, and I came to stay with you."

Jamey has been sick a lot lately. Mom says he has a kind of cancer called leukemia. This means that some of the cells in Jamey's blood aren't normal. They're growing too fast.

Grandma let me stay home from school. We played games, ate lunch, and watched TV. Mom and Dad called on the telephone, but they could only talk for a few minutes. It was almost bedtime before Dad finally came home, alone.

"Hello, Brian," he said, putting his arm around my shoulders. He looked very sad.

"Is Jamey okay?" I asked.

"No," Dad said softly. "Jamey is very sick. Mom wants to stay with him in the hospital so he won't be alone."

Dad slowly sat down. I touched his hand, but he didn't look up. I was frightened.

"Is Jamey going to die?" I asked.

"I don't know. The doctors are going to try everything they can so he won't," Dad said.

That night I stayed up with Dad and Grandma until Mom called. She said Jamey was out of danger. "I'll try to call you again before school tomorrow," she told me.

But Mom didn't call in the morning, and Dad said I had to go to school, anyway. It was hard to listen to my teacher when all I could think of was my brother. Was he in pain? What were the doctors doing to him? Why hadn't Mom called me this morning? Didn't she know I was worried? *I'm* her son, too!

When I got home, Grandma met me at the door. "How would you like to see Jamey?" she said. "I just talked to your mother on the phone. She said Jamey's better, and if we hurry, we can make the visiting hours."

Grandma carried a bag to the car. She had packed a change of clothes for Mom. "Your mother is going to stay a few more days with Jamey," she explained.

Even though Jamey had been in the hospital before, I had never been there. It looked scary from the parking lot. I didn't want to go in, but Grandma pulled me along.

Inside the lights were bright, and everything looked clean and shiny. It smelled like the medicine Mom puts on cuts.

A nurse named Nancy took us to Jamey's room. By the door was a table with paper clothes and masks. Nancy showed me how to put on a gown and cover my nose and mouth with a mask.

"Everyone has germs," she told us. "They don't bother people who are healthy. But Jamey is very sick, and your germs could make him worse."

Jamey's hospital room was small, with a big TV high on a shelf. There was a baseball game on. Mom was there, wearing a gown and mask like Grandma and me.

Jamey looked tiny in the hospital bed. He smiled when he saw me, and I smiled back. But I don't think he could tell because of my mask.

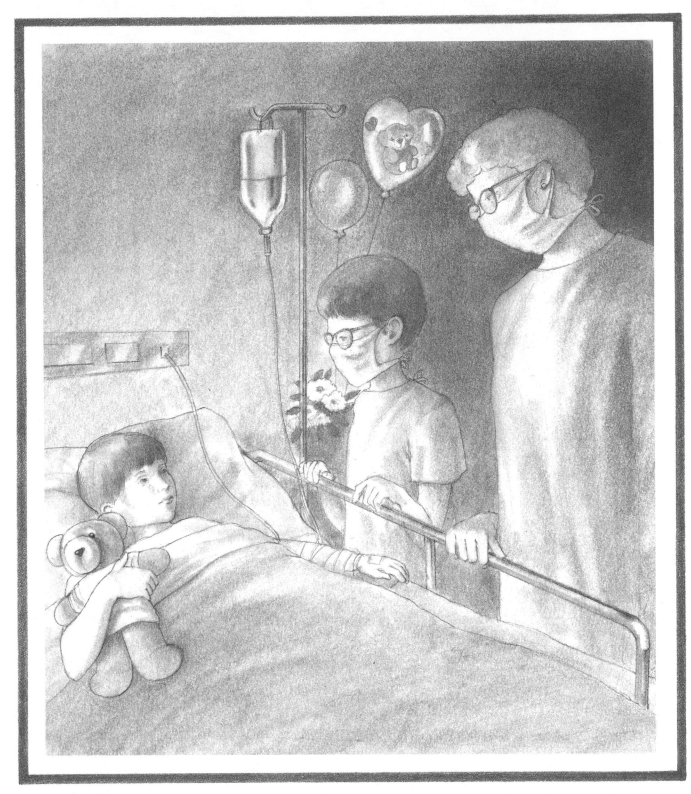

One of Jamey's arms was taped to a board and lay flat beside him. A tube ran from his arm to an upside-down bottle that hung from a pole. I could see liquid dripping into the tube. Even though I wasn't close to the pole, Mom said, "That's the IV—don't bump it. We hope that the medicine going into Jamey's arm will make him well."

Nancy came into the room with a needle, tube, and cotton. "It's time to check your blood cells, Jamey," she said.

Jamie held up his finger.

"This will be your last finger stick," Nancy said. "This afternoon we'll put a device in the back of your hand to draw blood from. Then you won't get poked for each test."

I watched Jamey's blood go up a skinny tube. "I'll check this right away," Nancy said.

Jamey didn't cry when his finger was pricked. "Didn't that hurt?" I asked him.

"A little," he said, closing his eyes. He didn't seem to care about anything.

"Jamey, don't sleep yet. I brought you some of my baseball cards," I said, holding them up for him to see. "You can have my old-timer cards. Look, here's Joe Garagiola, the catcher you've always wanted."

Jamey didn't answer.

"He's very tired," Mom said. "I'm glad you came to visit, but I think it's time to go now."

Jamey didn't come home for a whole week. I hardly ever saw Mom and Dad. When they weren't at the hospital, they were at work. It seemed as if they had forgotten me.

"Don't feel bad, Brian," Grandma said. "In a few days, Jamey will be home, and everything will be normal."

But after Jamey came home, things were *not* normal.

"Don't play so rough with Jamey," Mom said.

"Cover your mouth when you cough," Dad said. "You could pass your germs onto Jamey."

Even Grandma cared more for Jamey than for me. "Pick up your toys, Brian dear," she said. "We can't have Jamey tripping over them."

Nobody paid any attention to how *I* felt.

"I wish I had cancer!" I shouted one day. "Then maybe you'd care if I got a cold or fell and hurt myself. If I was sick, maybe you'd spend time with me instead of going to work."

Mom knelt down and looked into my eyes. "Don't ever say that," she said sadly. "I couldn't bear to have you so sick." She held me tightly. "I love you, Brian," she said. "I'll try to be around more for you."

Mom and Dad did try to spend more time with me, and for a while things were better around our house. Jamie seemed like the same old kid. But then something strange happened. When he combed his hair, big clumps fell out.

Mom said, "That's a side effect of chemotherapy. The medicine that was in the IV can cause hair to fall out."

Before long, Jamey was completely bald. "Just call me Joe Garagiola," he said, grinning.

In a week, Jamie had to return to the hospital for a radiation treatment. When it was time to go, he began to cry. "I don't want to go to the hospital anymore!" he said.

"No needles this time," Mom told him, "and if you want, Brian can go with us."

Jamey smiled a little. "Okay," he said with a sigh.

The next day I went with Mom and Jamey to the hospital. I held my brother's hand as we walked down the hall. A technician greeted us in the radiology department. "Dr. Barnes feels Jamey must have radiation to destroy the bad cells in his body," the man explained.

"Will it hurt?" I asked.

"No. It's something like getting an X-ray. It's not painful, but Jamey will have to hold very still."

The man took Jamey into a small room and had him lie on a high table. Above Jamey was a big machine that hung from the ceiling. Mom and I had to wait outside. After the door was closed, we watched Jamey on a special TV.

Later, at home, Jamey said, "That didn't hurt a bit." But he fell asleep without eating supper.

When Jamey didn't get stronger, Mom and I went back with him to the hospital. After testing his blood again, Dr. Barnes told us that Jamey had to stay in the hospital until he was better.

That night before I went to bed, I told Grandma that I would do anything to help Jamey. When I fell asleep, I dreamed that Jamey and I were playing baseball with Mom and Dad in a grassy field, like we used to do before he got sick.

In the middle of the night, I woke up. Mom and Dad were sitting on my bed. Mom was crying.

"Jamey needs your help, Brian," she said. "The medicine and radiation aren't enough to make him well. He needs a bone-marrow transplant, and he needs it from you."

"What's a bone-marrow transplant?" I asked.

"The doctor wants to take some of the good cells from deep inside your hipbone and put them into Jamey," Dad said. "Both Mom and I tried to give our cells, but the doctor thinks yours would match Jamey's best because you are a part of Mom and me, just like Jamey."

Then he showed me a bandage over his hipbone. "This is where they take the marrow from," he said.

I was afraid. What if the transplant really hurt and never stopped hurting? What if they accidentally gave me Jamey's cells, and I got sick like him? I didn't want to die!

Mom and Dad must have guessed how scared I was. "You can't get cancer by giving him some of your bone marrow," Dad said.

"The doctors will put you to sleep so you won't feel any pain," added Mom, "although your hip may be a little sore when you wake up."

"The operation may not work," Dad said gently.

"Do you mean I could do this and Jamey might die, anyway?" I asked.

Dad nodded. "But the doctor says if your cells match Jamey's, you are the best chance he has of living."

I loved Jamey, and I wanted him to get better. I was afraid, but I had to try. "I'll do it," I told Mom and Dad.

Mom called the doctor to tell him I was coming to the hospital. Grandma helped me pack a little bag. "You are the bravest boy in the world," she said.

Dr. Barnes met Mom, Dad, and me in my hospital room. He listened to my heart, and a nurse took some of my blood. If it didn't match Jamey's, I couldn't help.

"You appear to be a perfect match!" Dr. Barnes said in a little while when he came back to my room. "We need to do the transplant right away. We'll examine your bone marrow, and if it's right, we'll give it to Jamey immediately. I'll make sure everything's ready for you." He rushed from the room.

Mom walked beside the cart that took me down to surgery. We stopped outside Jamey's room. "Thank you, Brian," he called, too weak to wave.

The nurses pushed my cart to the operating room. Mom wasn't allowed to go farther. She kissed my cheek. "I hope this works," I said nervously.

"Here's our hero!" Dr. Barnes called when I entered the operating room. He had a mask on, but I recognized his voice. "I'm going to give you some medicine that will let you sleep. Start counting and see how far you get."

I only remember counting to twelve.

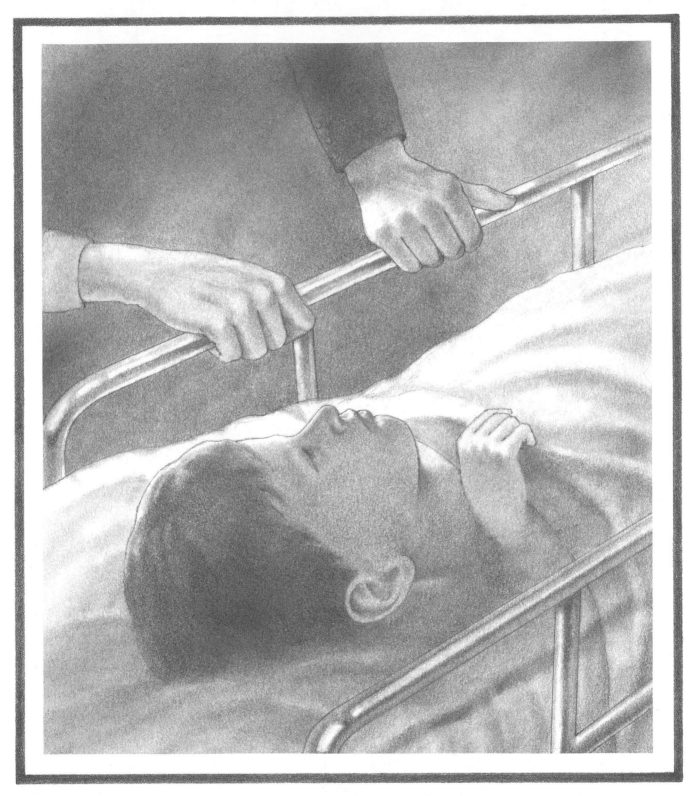

When I woke up, Nancy was taking me back to my room. "You did great, Brian!" she said. On my hip was a thick bandage.

Grandma and Mom were waiting in my room. After lunch, when I felt strong enough, they helped me dress. "You can visit Jamey before you go home," Mom said.

Dad was sitting by Jamey's bed. He was watching the tube leading to Jamey's wrapped arm.

"Are my cells in there?" I asked.

"Yes," Dad said proudly. "And I do believe that Jamey is stronger already!"

"How do you feel?" Jamey asked me.

"Like I slid hard into home plate," I admitted.

But I didn't mind. Because of that little bit of me in Jamey, he may come home, to stay.

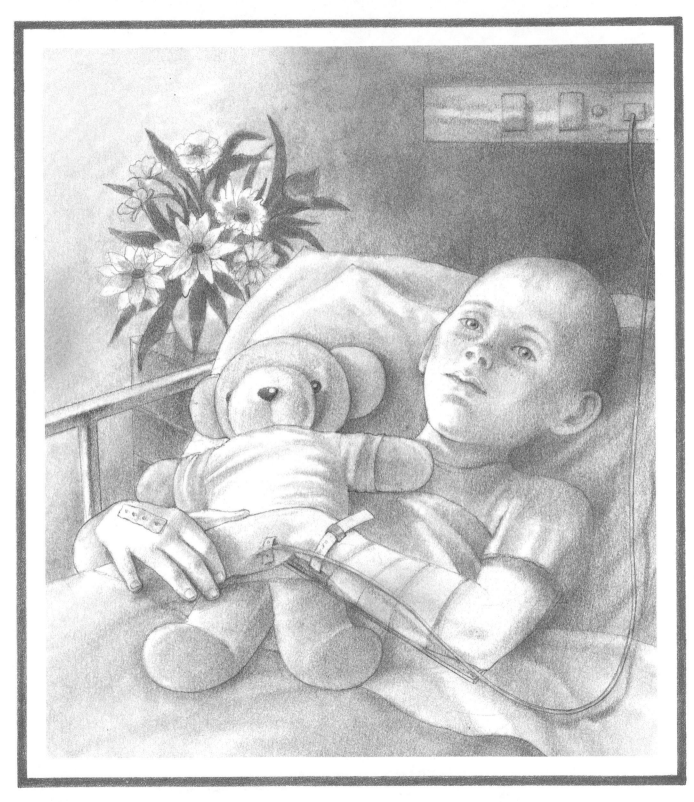